To Clare and Amy,
lots of love
D.W.

Fizz the shy fire engine

Scoop the boastful digger

Chug the helpful tractor

Choo the forgetful train

ORCHARD BOOKS
96 Leonard Street, London EC2A 4XD
Orchard Books Australia
32/45-51 Huntley Street, Alexandria, NSW 2015
ISBN 1 84121 484 1 (hardback)
ISBN 1 84362 284 X (paperback)
First published in Great Britain in 2003
First paperback publication in 2004
Text and illustrations © David Wojtowycz 2003
The right of David Wojtowycz to be identified as the author
and illustrator of this work has been asserted by him in accordance
with the Copyright, Designs and Patents Act, 1988.
A CIP catalogue record for this book is available from the British Library.
(hardback) 10 9 8 7 6 5 4 3 2 1
(paperback) 10 9 8 7 6 5 4 3 2 1
Printed in Hong Kong, China

FIZZ
the Fire Engine!

David Wojtowycz

little 🌳 ORCHARD

Fizz the fire engine wanted
to be a brave hero.

whee-ow, whee-ow!

He loved racing to the rescue.

And he loved his super long ladder.

But Fizz was shy. He thought his siren was too noisy and he never EVER flashed his light.

So he was always
last to arrive at the rescue.

Until one day . . . *bring!* *bring!* *bring!*

The alarm bell at the station rang.
A TRAIN IS STUCK IN THE TUNNEL!

Fizz revved up his
engine and rushed off.

What a dark and scary tunnel!
Bravely, Fizz raced in.

Oh no! Chuff the goods train had run out of fuel. "We need more help," said Fizz.

Clickety-clack, Clickety-clack!
went the track.
Hooray! Help was coming.

"Choo! Choo!"
came a noise.

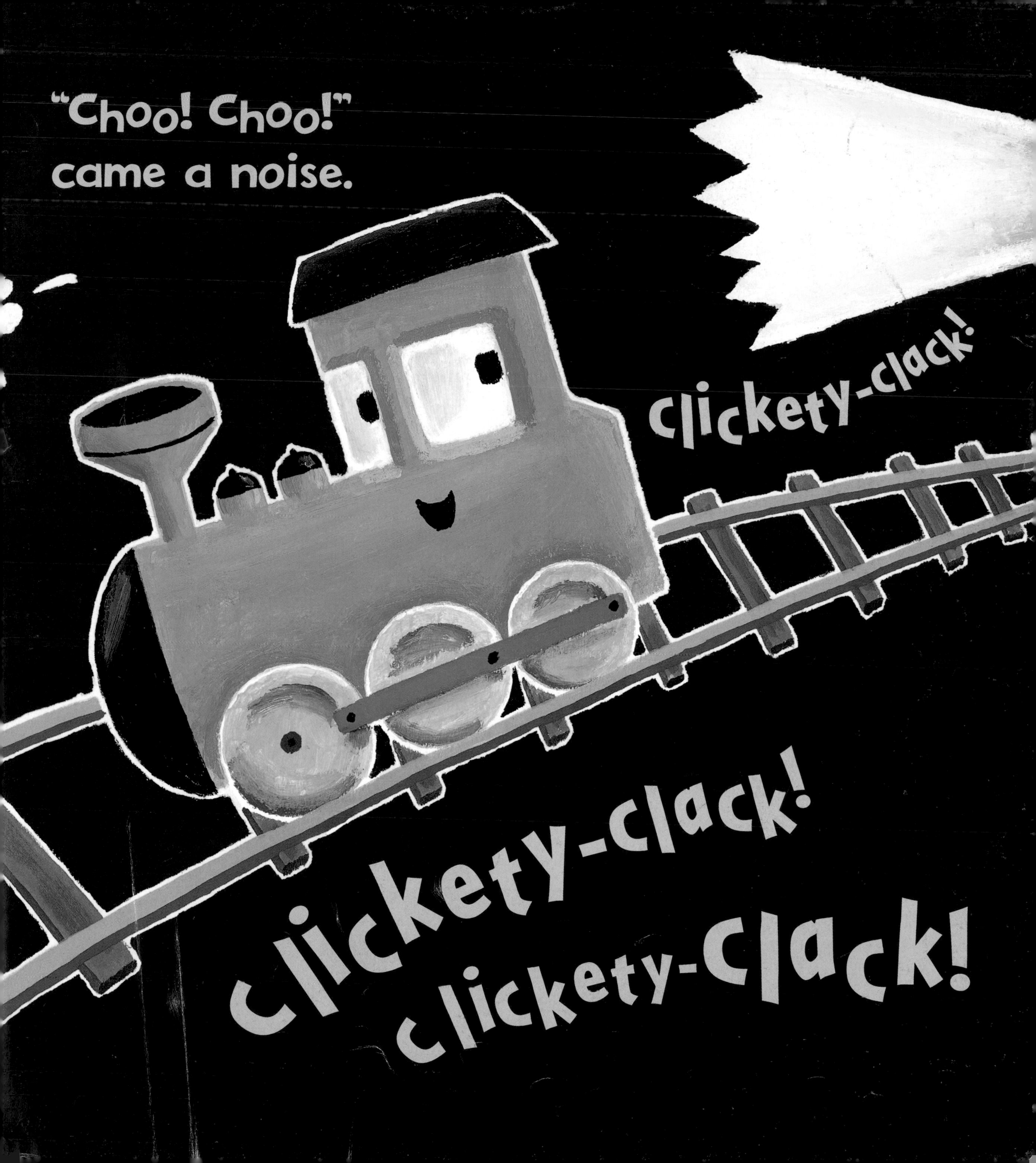

It was Choo
the train . . .

but he wasn't coming to the rescue.
He was speeding into town.

There was going to be a crash!

"STOP!" cried Fizz,
but Choo couldn't hear him.

nee-nar, nee-nar!

flash flash flash!

nee-nar!

nee-nar!

Yes, he was!

Choo slammed on his brakes.

But he was getting closer and closer.

s-c-r-e-e-c-h!

He slammed harder, and stopped – just in time!

With Choo's help, Chuff was soon pushed out of the tunnel. "Phew! Well done Fizz," said Choo. "You're our hero!"

From then on, Fizz wasn't a shy fire engine any more. And when he raced to the rescue, he ALWAYS made a lot of noise.

nee - nar!